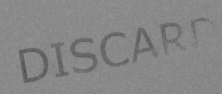

To all the wobbly ones—PG

For Deb—BW

Little Hare Books
an imprint of
Hardie Grant Egmont
Ground Floor, Building 1, 658 Church Street
Richmond, VIC 3121, Australia

www.littleharebooks.com

Text copyright © Phillip Gwynne 2012
Illustrations copyright © Bruce Whatley 2012

First published 2012
Reprinted in 2012

Cataloguing-in-Publication details are available from the National Library of Australia

978 1 921714 59 7 (hbk.)

Designed by Vida & Luke Kelly
Produced by Pica Digital, Singapore
Printed through Phoenix Offset
Printed in Shen Zhen, Guangdong Province, China, June 2012

6 5 4 3 2

The Queen with the Wobbly Bottom

by **Phillip Gwynne**
& illustrated by **Bruce Whatley**

LITTLE HARE
www.littleharebooks.com

There once was a queen,
a beautiful and clever queen,
who was loved throughout her land.

But when she looked in the mirror,
when she wriggled her hips,
her bottom wobbled
just like a raspberry jelly.

'My people can't love me,' said the Queen.

'But they do!' said the Royal Lady-In-Waiting.

'My people must make fun of me,' said the Queen.

'But they don't!' said the Royal Lady-In-Waiting.

'Listen!' said the Queen. 'Listen to what they're saying: "Wobbly, wobbly, see how it wobbles."'

A notice appeared on the palace wall.

> *To whoever can solve*
> *the problem of the royal wobble,*
> *Her Majesty, Queen of this Land,*
> *offers a thousand golden coins.*

The Beautician knocked on the palace door.

'Rub this cream on the wobbly area,' he said. 'And after thirty days there'll be no more wobble.'

'Yuck!' said the Queen. 'It looks horrible.'

'Blaah!' said the Queen. 'It smells horrible.'

But every night the Queen rubbed the horrible cream all over her wobbly bottom.

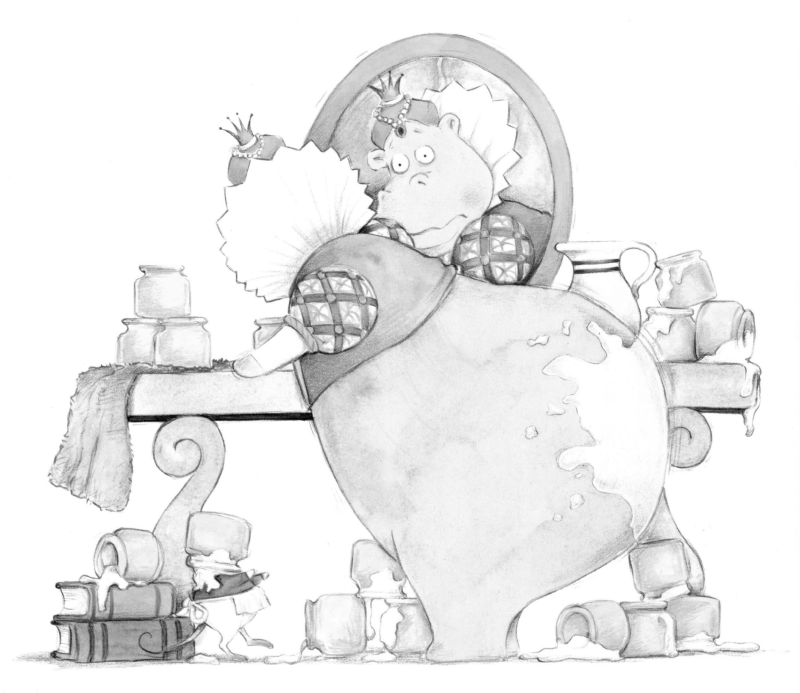

After thirty days her bottom had
no warts, pimples or carbuncles.

She looked in the mirror.

She wriggled her hips.

Her bottom still wobbled
just like a raspberry jelly.

'Throw the Beautician
into the deepest dungeon,'
ordered the Queen.

A new notice appeared on the palace wall.

This time the Queen offered five thousand golden coins.

The Inventor knocked on the palace door.

'To dewobble the royal bottom,' said the Inventor, 'you need to sit in the Dewobbiliser for one hour every day for thirty days.'

The Queen sat in the Dewobbiliser.

The Dewobbiliser shook.

The Dewobbiliser rattled.

The Queen shook.

The Queen rattled.

After thirty days the Queen's teeth
were loose and her knees knocked.

She looked in the mirror.

She wriggled her hips.

Her bottom still wobbled
like a raspberry jelly.

'Throw the Inventor
into the deepest dungeon,'
ordered the Queen.

A new notice appeared on the palace wall.

This time the Queen offered ten thousand golden coins.

The Fitness Instructor knocked on the palace door.

'Thirty days on this program,' he said, 'will knock the royal gluteus maximus back into shape.'

The Queen did push-ups and pull-ups.

She swam and she ran.

She did high-impact, low-impact
and no-impact aerobics.

After thirty days she could swim like a
dolphin. She could run like a rabbit.

She looked in the mirror.

She wriggled her hips.

Her gluteus maximus still
wobbled like a raspberry jelly.

'Throw the Fitness Instructor
into the deepest dungeon,'
ordered the Queen.

A new notice appeared on the palace wall.

This time it said,

> **To whoever can solve
> the problem of the royal wobble,
> Her Majesty, Queen of this Land,
> offers her hand in marriage.**

The Poet knocked on the palace door.

'I bring no special cream,' he said.
'No workout, no Dewobbilising machine.
But each day I will compose a poem
For Your Majesty to read
And after thirty days
The royal wobble will no longer trouble thee.'

'What a silly little man,' said the Queen.
'Throw him into the deepest dungeon.'

More men knocked on the palace door.

There were tricksters with lotions and swindlers with potions and quacks with pills of every colour.

But the royal bottom still wobbled just like a raspberry jelly.

'It's no good,' sighed the Queen.
'I've tried everything.'

'Not quite,' said the Royal Lady-In-Waiting.

'Okay, bring back that silly little man,' said the Queen.

Each night, high in a tower, by the light of a flickering candle, the Poet wrote a poem in praise of the Queen.

Each morning, as the sun rose, the Royal Lady-In-Waiting collected the poem.

Each evening the Queen sat on her balcony
and read the words the Poet had written.

After thirty days and thirty poems
the Queen looked in the mirror.

After thirty days and thirty poems
she wriggled her hips.

Her bottom still wobbled
just like a raspberry jelly.

But she didn't care.

The Poet adored her, wobbly bottom or not.

Her people loved her, wobbly bottom or not.

She was the Queen, wobbly bottom or not.

The Queen, true to her promise,
offered her hand in marriage.

But the Poet refused.

'Your Majesty,' he said, 'I can't marry you because I love another.'

The Queen breathed
a sigh of relief.

She didn't really want
to get married.

Especially not to such
a silly little man.

The Poet's first book, *Thirty Poems in Praise of our Queen*, became a bestseller.

He was famous throughout the land.

He was loved by all the people.

The Poet and the Royal Lady-In-Waiting
lived happily ever after.

And so did the Queen.